Bears at the Beach

Emma Carlisle

Macmillan Children's Books

Today we went on an adventure.

Dad packed a parasol, Mum rolled a giant towel, and I brought my brand new kite.

I couldn't wait to fly it!

And even though I was excited,

I sat still and didn't wriggle,

as me, Mum and Dad all went to...

... the beach!

"I'm going to lie down and read," said Mum.

But the beach is not for lying on, it's for playing on!

So that's what we did.

Then we went on a boat around the bay.

After lunch I couldn't wait
to fly my kite.

But Mum and Dad
said there was no wind
and I needed the wind
to help me.

But my kite wanted to fly, I could tell!
So I ran and ran as fast as I could.

"Mum, Dad, look!"

But when I turned around,
I couldn't see Mum and Dad
anywhere. I was lost!

They weren't by
the ice creams,

or by the
sandcastles,

and they weren't
having a swim.

I searched up high,

and I searched
down low.

I even searched round and round!

It was starting to feel cold
and I was getting hungry.
Some families started to
go home...

I wished I could
go home too.

Then suddenly,
I wasn't just lost...

But nobody on the beach could hear me, it was far too windy. "Go away wind!" I said.

But then I had
an idea!

It was a
very good idea.

"There he is!"
cried Mum and Dad.

"We've been looking
everywhere for you!"

"It looks like it was windy enough to fly your kite," said Dad.

"And we're very lucky it was," said Mum.

They said I was a very clever bear.

Dad packed up the parasol, Mum rolled up the giant towel,

and I told them all about my adventure.

Mum and Dad said I wasn't
to run off again, and I promised
I wouldn't.

I said "Being at the beach is
only fun when you are both
here with me."

Peep! Peep! "All aboard!"

It was getting very late, so we all had to run...

...and jump on the train!

I sat still and didn't wriggle,

as me, Mum and Dad went all the way...

home.